LOGIC PUZZLES

Mark Fowler

Illustrated by
Radhi Parekh

Designed by
Radhi Parekh and Sarah Dixon

Edited by
Sarah Dixon

Contents

Series Editor: Gaby Waters
Assistant Editor: Michelle Bates
Puzzle checkers: Christina Hopkinson and Rachel Bladon

Before You Start

Baffling brainteasers, cryptic sequences, strange conundrums, complex board games . . . all these and more lie in wait on the pages ahead. Every puzzle can be solved by logical deduction. Some are moderately tricky, while others could prove fiendishly difficult.

Look carefully at the documents and illustrations which accompany each puzzle. They contain all the information you need to find the solution. If you get stuck, turn to pages 42-44 for clues and hints on how to tackle the puzzles. You will find the answers on pages 45-48.

You can pick out a puzzle at random to solve, if you dare. But if you tackle them in order, you will discover several stories emerging, with a recurring cast of characters. Each story can be identified by its emblem and its heading, as shown on this double page.

There is more to these five stories than meets the eye, for buried in their midst is the strange tale of the seven lost statues of Alfresco. On page 44 there are hints to set you on the trail of these statues, but it is up to you to unravel the book's central mystery and locate their final hiding place.

Skarpa the Bold and the Weather Charm of Wailen Valla

Skarpa the Bold is a heroic adventurer from the northern land of Maelstrom. During the Dismal Age of Turmoil and Strife, raiders attack Maelstrom's shores and carry off a ship's figurehead known as the Weather Charm of Wailen Valla. Skarpa vows to recover the figurehead, for only this protects Maelstrom from the fierce storms which rage across the Northern Seas. His adventures have been pieced together using a selection of objects found inside an ancient longboat.

Carilla di Galliard and the Statue of the Cantador

Carilla di Galliard lives in Madrigola, a kingdom many miles south of Maelstrom, during the Merry Age of Minstrels. Almost all Madrigolans are fine musicians, but Carilla cannot sing or play a note. She is searching for a statue called the Cantador, for legend says that whoever finds this magic figure will become a great musician. Four tapestries from the Grand Palace of Madrigola illustrate Carilla's quest.

Peg Traherne and the Search for Obadiah Walrus

Peg Traherne is a secret agent living in the land of Wayward during the Swashbuckling Age of Buccaneers. Her latest mission is to track down Obadiah Walrus, the missing leader of a recently-formed group called the Society of Alfresco. The details of Peg's adventures are revealed in a bundle of papers found inside an old pirate fort in the distant Heliotropic Islands.

Percival Sharpe and the Faymus Treasures

One hundred and fifty years later, four valuable treasures are stolen from Faymus Towers, a large house in the middle of Cragge, Wayward's northernmost village. Renowned sleuth Percival Sharpe is called in to track down the thieves and recover the stolen treasures. Percival's investigations have been reconstructed using a selection of exhibits from Wayward Museum.

Freya de Fresque and the Alfrescan Casket

At the beginning of the Modern Age, the Society of Alfresco sends Madrigola's leading explorer, Freya de Fresque, to the eastern land of Magenta. Freya's mission is to retrieve the mysterious Alfrescan Casket from a secret hiding place. Her journey across Magenta is charted for the first time using the contents of an old chest from the society's headquarters.

The Seven Statues

The seven mysterious statues come from the island of Alfresco, and depict the gods of food, drink, jests, acrobatics, dance, poetry and music. Over a thousand years ago, they were stolen by a band of raiders called the Cafelors and ever since then the island has been stricken by disaster. The Society of Alfresco has vowed to find the statues and return them to Alfresco, in the belief that this will restore the island's good fortune. So far, the evil descendents of the Cafelors have thwarted them in their worthy quest, but now there is a chance to ensure the society's success for these pages contain all the information needed to track down the seven statues and bring in a new Alfrescan golden age.

Midnight Rendezvous

Acting on the instructions of the Society of Alfresco, secret agent Peg Traherne rides to an old castle on Wayward Moor. Here she must meet a contact who has information that will help her in her mission to find the society's missing leader, Obadiah Walrus. She knows that the castle is surrounded by members of the sinister Cafelors organization and her contact is trapped inside. One of the castle's entrances will be left unguarded after midnight. Peg must find the safe door so that she can meet her contact.

Which is the safe entrance?

Jonson not Ø - guarding either the Old Keep or the East Tower

The Society of Alfresco
October 13th

To Agent Traherne,

You must go to Castle Cloud on Wayward Moor to meet a contact who has information vital to your mission. The castle has been surrounded by seven members of a sinister organization called the Cafelors. They are guarding all seven entrances and your contact is trapped inside. However, one entrance will be left unguarded between midnight and one o'clock tonight, when a guard called Morgrim must contact his cronies in Marshby. You must discover which entrance Morgrim is guarding and slip inside the castle during his absence.

Morgrim's fellow guards are called Shark, Jonson, Graves, Smythe, Clipper and Hook. The seven are also known by the following symbols: Ω, Ψ, $\exists$, $\emptyset$, Σ, ∇ and $\wedge$. We don't know who has which symbol, except for Smythe who is Σ. Morgrim is not $\exists$, ∇ or $\emptyset$, and $\exists$ is not Shark, Jonson, or Graves. $\emptyset$ is not guarding the entrance to the Bell Tower, the Great Hall, or the North Tower, and neither Ψ nor ∇ are guarding the Old Keep.

We enclose the two lockets and four views of the castle. These contain all the other information we have been able to gather.

Good luck

The Bell Tower is not guarded by Hook or Morgrim

Cloud - North View

The Ghost Tower is not guarded by ∇ or $\exists$

Hook - not Ψ or $\emptyset$ - not guarding the East Tower or the Great Hall

Ω is guarding the East Tower

Castle Cloud - East

The Old Keep is not guarded by Clipper, Hook or Shark

Castle Cloud - South View

The Great Hall

Graves is guarding the North Tower

The South Tower is not guarded by ∇, $\exists$, or $\wedge$

Castle Cloud - West View

The Secret of the Symbols

At a great ceremony held on the feast day of the four-headed dragon, Skarpa the Bold vows to recover the stolen Weather Charm of Wailen Valla. Before he can begin his search, Skarpa has to seek the advice of Fjor, the wise enchanter. Fjor lives in the Hall of Fire and Ice across Maelstrom's hazardous northern wastes. With the help of this strange table of symbols, Skarpa must discover which five perilous places he will encounter on his way to the enchanter's hall.

What are the five places?

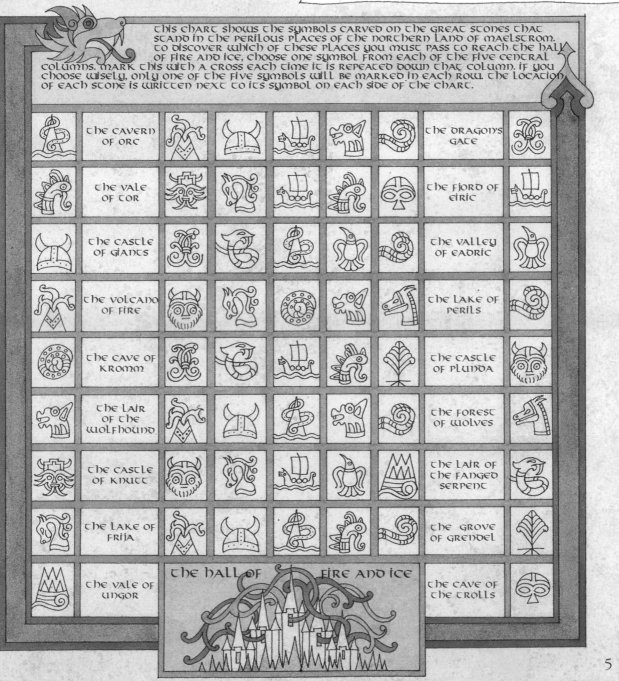

THIS CHART SHOWS THE SYMBOLS CARVED ON THE GREAT STONES THAT STAND IN THE PERILOUS PLACES OF THE NORTHERN LAND OF MAELSTROM. TO DISCOVER WHICH OF THESE PLACES YOU MUST PASS TO REACH THE HALL OF FIRE AND ICE, CHOOSE ONE SYMBOL FROM EACH OF THE FIVE CENTRAL COLUMNS. MARK THIS WITH A CROSS EACH TIME IT IS REPEATED DOWN THAT COLUMN. IF YOU CHOOSE WISELY, ONLY ONE OF THE FIVE SYMBOLS WILL BE MARKED IN EACH ROW. THE LOCATION OF EACH STONE IS WRITTEN NEXT TO ITS SYMBOL ON EACH SIDE OF THE CHART.

THE CAVERN OF ORC — THE DRAGON'S GATE

THE VALE OF TOR — THE FJORD OF EIRIC

THE CASTLE OF GIANTS — THE VALLEY OF EADRIC

THE VOLCANO OF FIRE — THE LAKE OF PERILS

THE CAVE OF KROMM — THE CASTLE OF PLUNDA

THE LAIR OF THE WOLFHOUND — THE FOREST OF WOLVES

THE CASTLE OF KNUTT — THE LAIR OF THE FANGED SERPENT

THE LAKE OF FRIJA — THE GROVE OF GRENDEL

THE VALE OF UNGOR — THE HALL OF FIRE AND ICE — THE CAVE OF THE TROLLS

5

A Cryptic Sequence

At the beginning of his investigation into the theft of the Faymus Treasures, renowned sleuth Percival Sharpe is sent a mysterious package. It contains a curious dial, a pictorial map covered with cryptic emblems and a letter addressed to one of the thieves. On reading the letter, Percival realizes that he can use the map and the dial to discover where the villains were staying on the night of the crime.

Where were they staying?

To: ⅀

Tomorrow you will receive a package from headquarters. It contains a dial and a map showing all the buildings in the village of Cragge. Each building on the map has an emblem that is divided into five sections. Each section contains a shape and a symbol. The symbols represent numbers, as shown on the dial.

Five of the emblems form a sequence. The first, second and fifth emblems of the sequence are:

You must identify the third and fourth emblems. To do this, first translate the symbols into numbers and then look for five number sequences which run from the first emblem to the fifth. The first sequence links the numbers in the triangles; the second links the numbers in the diamonds; the third links the numbers in the squares; the fourth links the numbers in the circles and the fifth links the numbers in the pentagons. Finally, the shapes themselves move around the five emblems in a strange but predictable way.

The building marked with the fourth emblem is your base for Operation Faymus. On December 30th, you must make contact with Ω at the base. On the night of the 31st, you and Ω will break into Faymus Towers and steal the Faymus Treasures, then return to the base to await further orders.

The dial sent to ⅀

A PICTORIAL MAP
of the village of
CRAGGE

The Mummers' Advice

This tapestry shows the five Mummers of Marcato, the most confusing band of performers in all Madrigola. One of the Mummers speaks the truth all the time. One tells nothing but lies. The other three tell a mixture of truth and lies.

When asked how to find the statue, I say: "You must take the road to the town of Tabor."

You say no such thing

You must take the road

to the city of Mandolin

Indeed you must take

the road to Mandolin

At the crossroads, you must go to Castle Gargoylia

You must go to the

Castle of Arc

You must not go to Castle Gargoylia

You must go to Castle Gargoylia

You must head either to

Tabor or to Mandolin

I always tell a mixture

of truth and lies

That is not true

If the bear is always truthful

the juggler tells nothing but lies

That is false

At the castle you must find the sage

The Drummer

always tells the truth

The piper tells nothing but lies

You must find the pageboy

You must

find the cook

(vertical text, right margin:) THE STATUE OF THE GOD OF ACROBATICS WAS MADE IN AGONDA VILLAGE

Carilla di Galliard sets off across the land of Madrigola in search of the statue of the Cantador. At a fork in the road she meets a band of entertainers called the Mummers of Marcato who offer her advice. This tapestry shows their confusing suggestions. Carilla must find out which of their statements are truthful and so discover what to do next.

What should Carilla do?

The Route to the Amethyst Cave

Explorer Freya de Fresque sets off for the distant land of Magenta to retrieve the valuable Alfrescan Casket on behalf of the Society of Alfresco. At the Magentan port of Lapis Lazuli she collects a battered envelope containing a mysterious Magentan chart and an old letter.

Turmeric

Azira

Kesar

Caraway

Haldi

Bergamot

Tarragon

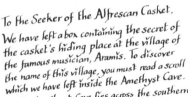

To the Seeker of the Alfrescan Casket,

We have left a box containing the secret of the casket's hiding place at the village of the famous musician, Aramis. To discover the name of this village, you must read a scroll which we have left inside the Amethyst Cave.

+ The Amethyst Cave lies across the southern marshlands of Magenta.

+ When you are crossing the marshes, you must always keep to the tracks.

+ Avoid the forests of Jakal, Sesame and Tyre, the mountains of Zephyr and Djinni, and the shores of Lake Laq, for all of these six places are inhabited by savage beasts and ruthless bandits.

The map enclosed with this letter will help you plot your route to the cave. You must use the information below the chart to locate the six perilous places.

Good luck

This chart of the Southern Marshlands of Magenta shows the tracks that link the region's mountain ranges, forests and lakes with the Amethyst Cave and the port of Lapis Lazuli
It takes five days to walk along each path shown on the map
The Forest of Sesame is five days' walk from Lake Laq
Lake Tirin is five days' walk from the Forest of Tyre
The Forest of Okra is five days' walk from the Mountains of Nadir
The Djinni Mountains are five days' walk from Lake Aral

According to the letter, a piece of vital information about the casket's hiding place has been left in the Amethyst Cave far across Magenta's treacherous southern marshes. Using the map, Freya must plot a safe route to the cave avoiding this region's six most hazardous landmarks.

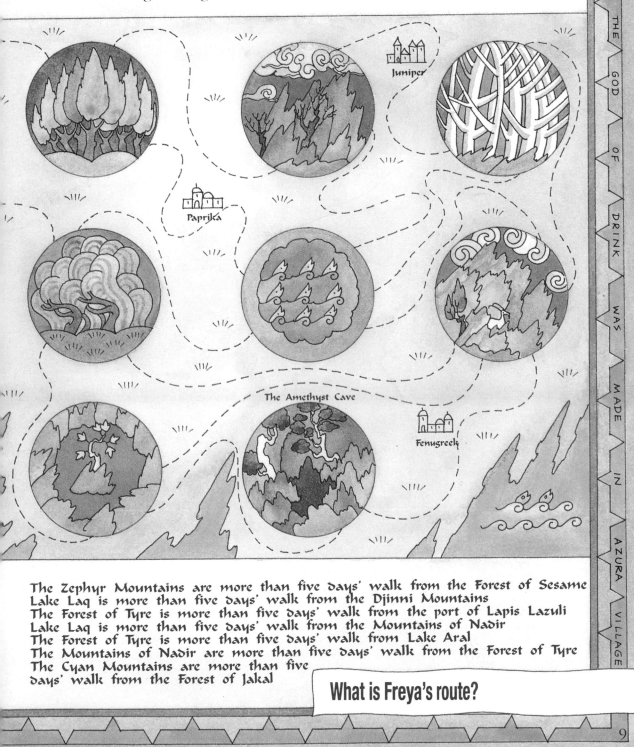

The Zephyr Mountains are more than five days' walk from the Forest of Sesame
Lake Laq is more than five days' walk from the Djinni Mountains
The Forest of Tyre is more than five days' walk from the port of Lapis Lazuli
Lake Laq is more than five days' walk from the Mountains of Nadir
The Forest of Tyre is more than five days' walk from Lake Aral
The Mountains of Nadir are more than five days' walk from the Forest of Tyre
The Cyan Mountains are more than five days' walk from the Forest of Jakal

What is Freya's route?

The Enigma of the Runik Isles

ON THIS MY CUNNING CHART I SHOW THE SIX ISLANDS OF THE RUNIK PEOPLE. ON EACH ISLAND THERE ARE SIX VILLAGES, AND EACH VILLAGE HAS BEEN GIVEN A SECRET SIGN. FOR EACH VILLAGE, I SHOW FOUR SIGNS BUT ONLY ONE SIGN IS THE VILLAGE'S TRUE SIGN AND THE OTHER THREE ARE FALSE SIGNS. NO TWO VILLAGES ON THE SAME ISLAND SHARE THE SAME TRUE SIGN. NO VILLAGE THAT SHARES ITS FLAG WITH ANY OTHER VILLAGE IN THE RUNIK ISLES WILL SHARE THAT OTHER VILLAGE'S TRUE SIGN.

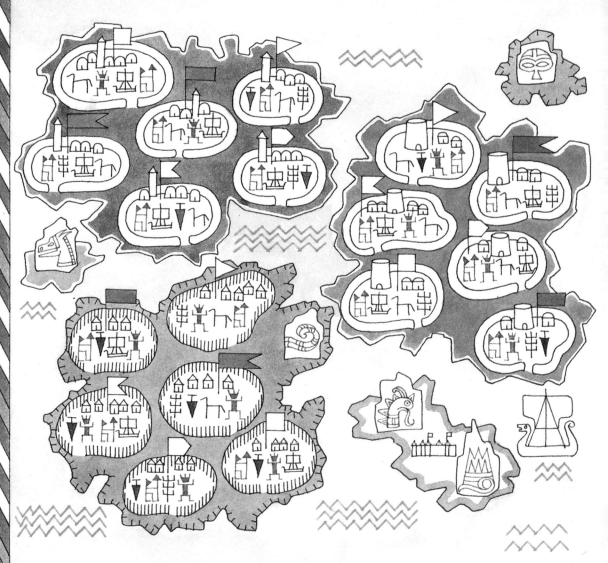

According to Fjor the Enchanter, the Weather Charm of Wailen Valla was stolen by the Warriors of the Whirlwind. These fearsome raiders come from the Isle of Doom Laiden, far across the windswept Western Seas. The only person who can guide Skarpa to this island is an explorer called Seega the Seafarer who lives in the village of Kamott in the Runik Isles.

To help Skarpa find Seega's village, the enchanter presents him with a talisman and a map of the Runik Isles. None of the villages is named on this map. Instead each one is identified by a flag and a symbol. Kamott's flag and symbol are carved on the talisman, but can Skarpa locate the village on the map?

Which village is Kamott?

The Riddle of the Knights

Carilla's search for the statue of the Cantador leads her to the Great Tournament of Madrigola. Here she learns that she must seek the help of Sir Jules Hautboys. Sir Jules is one of ten knights competing in the tournament. This tapestry shows the knights and all the details that Carilla can discover about them. By piecing this information together, she is able to identify Sir Jules.

This is the horse of Sir Gawain

The horse of Sir Caspar

The owner of this shield has a horse with red reins

This valiant knight has a horse with red reins

Sir Emilio

Sir Almeric and his horse

The owner of this shield has a horse with red reins

This scene shows the ten knights who fought at the great tournament of Madrigola, together with their horses and shields. Sir Gerard's horse has a great plume. The shields of Sir Almeric and Sir Jules are different shapes, but they have the same design. Sir Gerard's shield has a cross. Sir Sigismund has a black horse while the horse of Sir Balthus is white as snow. The champion of the joust is Sir Fernando the Flamboyant.

The owner of this shield rides a white horse

Sir Harold

Which knight is Sir Jules?

The Albatross Conundrum

At the castle, secret agent Peg Traherne learns that she must go to a ship called the Albatross, anchored at the port of Great Rigging. The Society of Alfresco's missing leader, Obadiah Walrus, was a passenger aboard this ship on its last voyage across the Southern Seas, but he never reached his destination. The details of his fate are recorded in the log book of the Albatross. This has been hidden in a barrel on the deck commanded by Lieutenant Draconio. Using an old plan of the ship and a mysterious letter, Peg must identify Draconio's deck.

We will set sail on August 11th with a valuable cargo consisting of five treasures: the Casket of Magenta, the Tamarind Jewels, the Galliard Lute, the Calypso Figure and the Goldenhall Talisman. Each of these treasures is to be stored on a different deck.

Neither Windlass nor Bosun will command the Gun Deck, for they are useless in a fight.

The Galliard Lute is not to be stored on the Lower Deck.

The spare sails are not to be stored on the Poop Deck.

Neither the Goldenhall Talisman nor the Galliard Lute will be on Bosun's deck, nor will they be stored on Draconio's deck.

Windlass will not command the Main Deck.

The Casket of Magenta is to be stored on the Gun Deck.

Castle Cloud
October 13th

To Agent Traherne,
Obadiah Walrus was a passenger on the Albatross when he disappeared. The ship's log book contains clues to Mr Walrus's fate, but the book has been hidden by the ship's officers, Lts Draconio, Bosun, Scurvy, Kraken and Windlass. I have discovered that the hiding place is a large barrel on the deck commanded by Draconio. I enclose an old plan of the Albatross with notes added by the captain before the ship's last voyage. These should enable you to identify Draconio's deck and find the log book.

Your
Contact

Scurvy will either command the deck where the Casket of Magenta is to be stored, or the deck where the Tamarind Jewels are to be stored. The other treasures are too valuable to entrust to his care.

Neither the ship's biscuits nor the firearms will be on Kraken's desk.

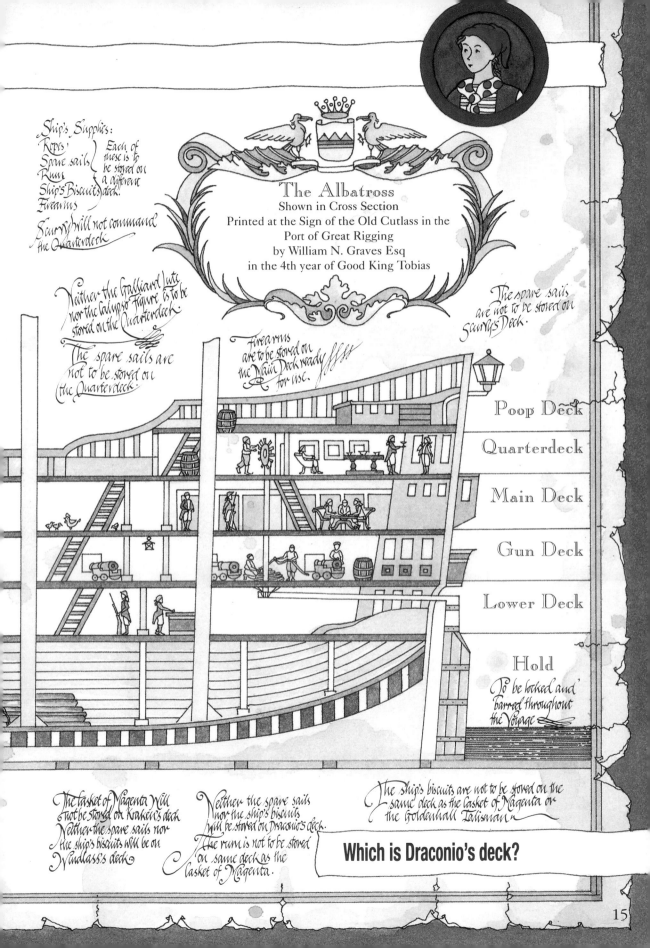

Ship's Supplies:
Ropes
Spare sails — Each of these is to be stored on a different deck.
Rum
Ship's Biscuits
Firearms

Scurvy will not command the Quarterdeck.

The Albatross
Shown in Cross Section
Printed at the Sign of the Old Cutlass in the
Port of Great Rigging
by William N. Graves Esq
in the 4th year of Good King Tobias

Neither the Galliard Lute nor the Calypso Figure is to be stored on the Quarterdeck.

The spare sails are not to be stored on the Quarterdeck.

Firearms are to be stored on the Main Deck ready for use.

The spare sails are not to be stored on Scurvy's Deck.

Poop Deck

Quarterdeck

Main Deck

Gun Deck

Lower Deck

Hold
To be locked and barred throughout the voyage

The Casket of Magenta will not be stored on Kraken's deck. Neither the spare sails nor the ship's biscuits will be on Windlass's deck.

Neither the spare sails nor the ship's biscuits will be stored on Draconio's deck. The rum is not to be stored on same deck as the Casket of Magenta.

The ship's biscuits are not to be stored on the same deck as the Casket of Magenta or the Goldenhall Talisman.

Which is Draconio's deck?

15

Ten Suspects

The Marchioness of Rotunda and her brother who left together on January 4th

DODO

FUGIT TEMPUS NON

Pursuing my enquiries into the theft of the Faymus Treasures, I have gathered the following information:
– the thieves were staying at the Dodo Club in the village of Cragge on the night of the crime
– five members of the club were staying there that night, and each had a guest with them
– each member left with his or her guest on a different day
– all ten people went straight to the town of Marshby where they stayed overnight
– two members left with their guests by train (one on the Gantry Express, the other on the Piston Express) while the others left with their guests by road (one in a carriage, one in a hansom cab, the third by stagecoach)
– the journey from Cragge to Marshby takes two days by road and one day by train
– according to the innkeeper of the Swan Inn in Marshby, his guests for the first fortnight in January included a man and a woman who arrived with a large chest bearing the Faymus crest. They must be the thieves.

Dear Mr. Sharpe,
Here is a list of members who stayed at the Dodo Club on the night of December 31st.
The Marchioness of Rotunda,
Mr. Jacob Spratt,
Mr. Robert Johnson,
Miss Lucinda Eliot,
Mr. Charlie Bounder.
These are the names of their guests.
(Unfortunately I cannot remember which guest came with which member.)
Miss Fanny Wren,
Mr. Denholm Hazzlitt,
Mr. Jonathon Sutch,
Miss Maria Jones,
Miss Priscilla Prince.
I also enclose several items which were left at the club. These may assist you in your investigation.
Your humble servant,
Francis Major de Mean,
General Steward of the Dodo Club

Fob watch belonging to suspect who left Cragge on January 2nd

BENSON'S REMEDIES
Hair Tonic
For lustrous locks

Hot on the trail of the thieves of the Faymus treasures, Percival Sharpe arrives at the headquarters of the exclusive Dodo Club. He knows that the thieves were among ten people staying at the club on the night of the crime. With the help of the club's steward, he gathers a bewildering assortment of information about the movements of all ten people. Once all the facts are pieced together, he will know which of the ten are the thieves.

This letter arrived on January 2nd, the day after Mr Sutch left Cragge

J. Sutch Esq,
c/o The Dodo Club,
Cragge Village

Opera glasses belonging to suspect who left Cragge on January 7th

The owner of this bottle left Cragge on January 5th

Est. 1854
Harcourt's Hansom Cabs
Miss Fanny Wren left in a hansom, but not with Mr Charlie Bounder. Bounder left three days before Miss Prince

The suspect who went by the Piston Express did not leave on January 1st

FLOODS STRIKE MARSHBY

The historic town of Marshby was flooded on January 6th during a freak storm. Fifteen buildings had to be evacuated, including the 400 year-old Swan Inn. "Our rooms were knee deep in water," said the inn's proprietor, Mr Jeremiah Drake. "We could not reopen for business until January 8th."

MARCHIONESS BECOMES GRAND DODO

At a lavish ceremony at the Dodo Club on December 31st, the Marchioness of Rotunda was invested as the new Grand Dodo. Club member Robert Johnson gave an eloquent speech in which he described the Marchioness as "probably the greatest Dodo of all time".

NOTICE OF AUCTION

On February 1st an auction will take place at Nether Marshby Manor, home of the late Colonel Windermere. Among the items for sale is a plant stand fashioned from a statue known as the Acrostik Acrobat, which Colonel Windermere acquired during a visit to the land of Magenta.

G G T C

THE GREAT GANTRY TRAIN COMPANY

proudly announces the opening of a railway line between the village of CRAGGE and the historic town of MARSHBY.

Gone are the days when you had to wait for the once weekly stagecoach. Now you have a choice of two trains a week. Both the GANTRY EXPRESS and the PISTON EXPRESS race through the countryside at more than twice the speed of the stagecoach. If you choose to take the PISTON EXPRESS from CRAGGE to MARSHBY, you will leave one day after the stagecoach but arrive at your destination at exactly the same time. What is more, both our trains are furnished to the highest standards of luxury and elegance.

A SUPERLATIVE EXPERIENCE!

Historic Marshby

This suspect left on the Gantry Express, arriving at Marshby three days after Mr R. Johnson

Jacob Spratt Esq

Who are the thieves?

17

The Riddle of the Musicians

In the 23rd year of the reign of King Samerkand the Wise, nine visitors from the Society of Alfresco came to Magenta in search of the lost statue of Wine and Wassail. The ten musicians of Magenta held a concert to entertain the visitors.

This painting shows the musicians playing a stirring piece of music called the Kantador. The names of their villages are written on their music stands.

Lalik is at Izarin's left side.
Balbek is in the pavilion with the red flag.
Sulah is at Balbek's side.

Aramis and Faron are in the same pavilion, but are not next to one another.
If Korabeth wears a white turban, Balbek wears one too.
Qat is either in the front row of the pavilion with the red flag or in the front row of the pavilion with the yellow flag.
If Haliah has a cloak, Aramis has one too.
Haliah is at Raban's side.
Aramis wears a white turban, but only if Lalik wears a cloak.
Korabeth is in the pavilion with the yellow flag.

Bergamot Kesar Fenugreek

Paprika Turmeric

Juniper Caraway

Tarragon Azira Haldi

Inside the Amethyst Cave, Freya de Fresque finds a painting from an old Magentan manuscript. This depicts a gathering of ten musicians from the villages of Magenta. Freya knows that she must go to the village of the musician called Aramis. Here she must collect a box which contains the secret of the Alfrescan Casket's hiding place. To discover the name of this village, she has to find out which of the ten players in the painting is Aramis.

What is the name of the village?

The Pirates' Island

Secret agent Peg Traherne hides aboard the Albatross before it sets sail on its next voyage. From the ship's log book, she has discovered that Obadiah Walrus was captured by a ruthless band of pirates from one of the seven Heliotropic Islands. Once the Albatross reaches these islands, Peg plans to swim ashore to rescue the pirates' hapless captive. But first she must identify their island using a poster and an earlier entry in the log book.

The Runaatongs of the Heliotropic Islands

1 Short-Haired Runaatong *(found on either Jaspar or Salamander Isle)*
2 Silver Runaatong *(found on Jaspar, Solferino or Eastern Islands)*
3 Klamorus Runaatong *(found on Corallina Island)*
4 Bouncing Runaatong
5 Howling Runaatong *(not on Jaspar Island)*
6 Rufus Runaatong
7 Long-Tailed Runaatong *(not on Cinnabar Island)*

WANTED FOR PIRA

A reward of ONE THOUSAND GOLD SOVEREIGN awaits the person who can bring the dastardly, despicable and devious pirates of the Southern Seas to justice. The ruthless freebooters operate from the Fort of Skulls, stronghold built on the ruins of an ancient palace on one of the Heliotropic Isles.

Barebones Jake

Buccaneer Bess

14th February
During the great storm, the ship suffered terrible damage and for three weeks we drifted until at dawn this morning we sighted the Heliotropic Islands.
As the crew celebrated, I set out to explore the islands with Isaac Skew, the naturalist. We attempted to identify the islands, but this proved a difficult task. All seven islands are covered with dense jungle, but each has a distinguishing landmark. The first, which I identified as Solferino, has a grumbling volcano, while the second has vast mango groves. We found a hermitage on the third island, an ancient palace on the fourth and a ruined tower on the fifth. The interior of the sixth is largely swamp, and the seventh has strange standing stones. From old sailors' tales, I knew that neither the palace nor the tower were on Jaspar Island, and that neither the swamps nor the mango groves could be on Corallina. I also remembered that the standing stones are not on Cinnabar Island, Jaspar Island, the Isle of Parakeets or Eastern Island.
Isaac Skew told me that the Heliotropics are home to monkey-like creatures called Runaatongs, and that each island is home to a different species. With the help of Mr Skew's natural history book, we attempted to identify the Runaatongs that we glimpsed among the jungle foliage. We spotted a Bouncing Runaatong on the island with the palace. The runaatong that we saw on the isle of the swamps was not the Rufus or the Silver. The runaatong on the isle with the mango groves was not the Silver or the Howling. According to Mr Skew, if the Long-Tailed lives on Eastern Island, the Rufus will not be on the island with standing stones; and if the tower is on the Isle of Parakeets, the Long-Tailed will not be on the island with the mango groves.

21st June
It is over four months since we left the Heliotropics, and at last we have reached the Isle of Alfresco. Fierce winds whip its shores, grey clouds shroud its hills. It is indeed a gloomy and desolate place.

Corallina   Cinnabar   Isle   Eastern Island
Jasper Island   Solferino

Not on an island inhabited by runaatongs with spots.

Not on Eastern or Jaspar islands, or the Isle of Parakeets.

Hermitage of Marabout

Which is the pirates' island?

The Stone of Doom Laiden

The isle of Lilla Vaga. This island was not raided in the year of the midnight sun or the year of the storms. The year of the storms was not the year when the isle of Loki was raided.

Knut the Fearsome. This warlord did not raid the isle of Alfresco. He is not the owner of the south fort. He did not carry out his raid in the year of the mighty seamonster.

Gunhilde the Ruthless. This warlord carried out a violent raid in the year of the great curse.

The isle of Alfresco. This island was not raided in the year of the storms or the year of the great curse. It is a barren place and there was little to take back to the raider's stronghold, which is not the fort of Blackstone.

Erik the Mighty. This warlord is not the owner of the north fort or the fort of the Dragonstone. Neither he nor Harold the Hardy carried out their raid in the year of the midnight sun.

Accompanied by Seega the Seafarer, Skarpa the Bold crosses the stormy Western Seas to the Isle of Doom Laiden. This island is the home of the Warriors of the Whirlwind, the fearsome band of raiders who stole the Weather Charm of Wailen Valla. According to Seega, they are led by five ruthless warlords. Each year, a different warlord takes command of the warriors and carries out a raid on a different land.

THE YEAR OF THE HEROIC SEA VOYAGE. THE SPOILS FROM THE PLACE RAIDED IN THIS YEAR (NOT THE ISLE OF VIDAR) WERE TAKEN TO THE FORT OF HIGH TOWERS, THE NORTH FORT OR THE FORT OF THE DRAGONSTONE.

SOMBRIK THE PROUD. THIS WARLORD IS NOT THE OWNER OF THE SOUTH FORT. HE DID NOT RAID THE ISLE OF ALFRESCO.

THE YEAR OF THE MIGHTY SEAMONSTER. IN THIS YEAR THE SPOILS OF A GREAT RAID WERE TAKEN TO THE NORTH FORT.

THE FORT OF HIGH TOWERS. THE SPOILS FROM THE ISLE OF VIDAR WERE TAKEN TO THIS FORT, BUT NOT BY GUNHILDE THE RUTHLESS OR SOMBRIK THE PROUD.

THE LAND OF MAELSTROM. THIS LAND WAS NOT RAIDED BY HAROLD THE HARDY OR SOMBRIK THE PROUD. THE SPOILS WERE NOT TAKEN TO THE SOUTH FORT OR THE FORT OF BLACKSTONE.

Each warlord lives with their warriors in a great fort on Doom Laiden. Skarpa suspects that the Weather Charm is hidden in the fort of the warlord who led the raid on Maelstrom. To identify this fort, Skarpa must piece together the inscriptions on a great stone that the vain warlords have erected on the island's shore to celebrate their most recent adventures.

Which fort should Skarpa search?

The Riddle of the Ten Towers

Sir Jules Hautboys sends Carilla to the Plains of Pavanne to find Aurora the Guardian of Secrets, for only she knows the fate of the statue of the Cantador. The Guardian lives in one of the ten towers on the plains, while the other nine are inhabited by the evil Lords of Lamotte. Carilla must locate the Guardian's tower using Sir Jules's descriptions. The towers are shown on this tapestry together with the knight's information.

Which is the Guardian's tower?

Here are the ten towers of the Plains of Pavanne
The Tower of Belle is across the river from the Tower of Torment
The Tower of Rigadoon is across the river from the Tower of Four Winds, but only if the Tower of Rigadoon stands on a hilltop
The Tower of Bay has a flag with an eagle
The Tower of Four Winds is across the river from the Tower of Torment, but only if the Tower of Four Winds has a pointed doorway
The Tower of Four Winds has a flag with a cross

The Tower of Rooks is on an island, but not if the Tower of Four Winds has a pointed doorway

The Tower of Four Winds has a flag with a lion, but only if the Tower of Sighs is surrounded by trees

The Tower of the Guardian is on the same side of the river as the Tower of Eagles, but not if the Tower of Bay has a flag with a lion

The Tower of Sighs has more turrets than the Tower of Bay

The Tower of Eagles has fewer turrets than the Tower of the Guardian

The Tower of High Dudgeon has fewer turrets than the Tower of Eagles

The Tower of Belle stands on a hilltop

The Secret Handovers

After extensive inquiries, Percival Sharpe discovers that the thieves have left the country on a steamer belonging to the Kraken Shipping Company. At the company's ticket office at the port of Great Rigging, Percival is surprised to find a large parcel addressed to him. This contains a letter from an anonymous informer, together with a book and a collection of papers.

January 20th

To Mr Sharpe,

As you may have guessed, you are not dealing with an ordinary theft. The thieves are members of a sinister organization called the Cafelors. This organization has sent the thieves to four foreign cities. In each of the cities they will go to a secret rendezvous where they will hand over one of the Faymus Treasures to their accomplices. I have been able to gather information about the handovers and I have noted everything down on the documents enclosed with this letter.

Yours in haste,
An Informer

P.S. Do not attempt to find out who I am or how I have obtained this information.

THE CITY OF SAN SERIF

MARCATO MANSION

Z6

ADMIT ONE

Not in the city of Kastler. Not the handover point for treasure ♡

Hôtel Aurora

• Handover point

not to be confused with the Lady Aurora, a steamer which is also a handover point.

Treasure ♡ is to be handed over one month before treasure ◇

The City of Ehrhardt

Handover here two months before handover in Kastler

At a secret meeting on January 1st, the Grand Council of the Cafelors made the following decisions:

1. Σ and Ω will hand over treasures ♡, ♧, ♤ and ◇ to accomplices at four separate locations, all in different cities. The handovers will take place on the 28th of each month from January to April.

2. Ψ and $\triangle$ are highly congratulated on their success in tracing the Jesting Figure. They will now join Σ and Ω on Operation Faymus.

3. ♈ and ϕ will co-ordinate Operation Dancer. The operation will target the Dancing Figure, which has been out of our hands since the Heliotropic Fiasco 150 years ago.

According to Percival's informer, the thieves have been ordered to go to four foreign cities. At a secret location in each city they will hand over one of the stolen Faymus Treasures to their accomplices. With the help of the parcel's contents, Percival can find out the date and location of the handover for each of the treasures.

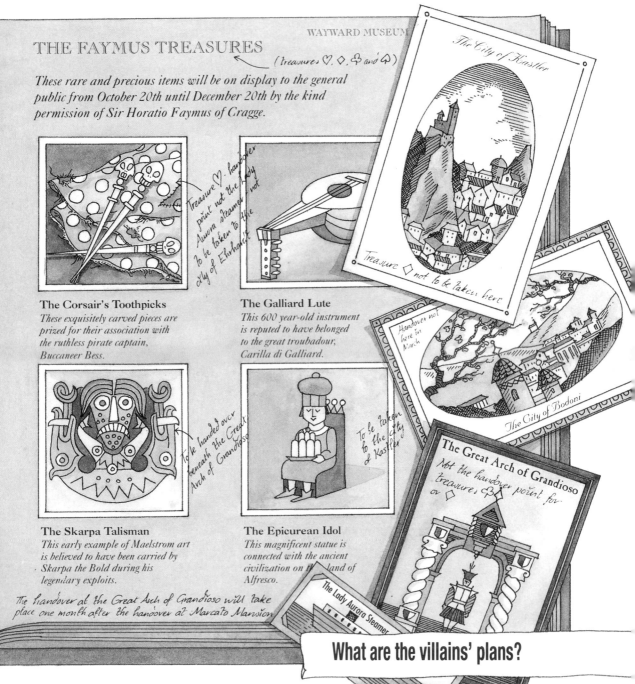

WAYWARD MUSEUM

THE FAYMUS TREASURES

(treasures ♡, ◊, ♧ and ♤)

These rare and precious items will be on display to the general public from October 20th until December 20th by the kind permission of Sir Horatio Faymus of Cragge.

The Corsair's Toothpicks
These exquisitely carved pieces are prized for their association with the ruthless pirate captain, Buccaneer Bess.

Treasure ♡. handover point not the Lady Aurora steamer not to be taken to the city of Ehrhaprist

The Galliard Lute
This 600 year-old instrument is reputed to have belonged to the great troubadour, Carilla di Galliard.

To be taken to the city of Kastler

The Skarpa Talisman
This early example of Maelstrom art is believed to have been carried by Skarpa the Bold during his legendary exploits.

To be handed over beneath the Great Arch of Grandioso

The Epicurean Idol
This magnificent statue is connected with the ancient civilization on the land of Alfresco.

The handover at the Great Arch of Grandioso will take place one month after the handover at Marcato Mansion

The City of Kastler

Treasure ◊ not to be taken here

Handover not here in March

The City of Bodoni

The Great Arch of Grandioso

Not the handover point for treasures ♧ or ◊

The Lady Aurora Steamer

What are the villains' plans?

A Game of Kaballo

To the Seeker of the Alfrescan Casket,

To locate the casket's hiding place, you must play our version of the ancient Magentan game of Kaballo.

+ The board is a coded map of Northern Magenta. The key to the main symbols is in a small panel to the left of the board.

+ The four pieces are called the Karray, the Rond, the Tri and the Lo-Zeng. Their moves and their starting positions are described in a large panel to the left of the board.

+ In our version of Kaballo, each piece makes four moves. They can only land on turquoise squares and no square can be landed on more than once.

+ When all four pieces are in their final positions, you must draw a line from the middle of the Karray's square to the middle of the Rond's square, then another line from the middle of the Tri's square to the middle of the Lo-Zeng's square.

+ The casket is hidden at the place where the two lines cross. You will find a clue to its exact location at the bottom of a dry well near this site.

Good luck

The Rond

This piece starts on square A13. For each turn, it moves in any of the eight ways shown here.

The Karray

This piece starts on square A6. For each turn, it moves in any of the eight ways shown here.

The Lo-Zeng

This piece starts on square A4. For each turn, it moves in any of the eight ways shown here.

The Tri

This piece starts on square A3. For each turn, it moves in any of the four ways shown here.

Mountain	Forest	Town
Lake	Village	Palace

The search for the Alfrescan Casket leads Freya de Fresque to a remote village in the heart of Magenta. When the villagers learn of Freya's mission, they bring her a small box containing a board and four pieces for a Magentan game called Kaballo, together with a pendant and a letter.

The letter explains that the brightly patterned board is a disguised map of Northern Magenta. If Freya moves the four Kaballo pieces around the board in a particular way, she will be able to locate the casket's hiding place.

Where is the casket hidden?

27

The Fort of Skulls

When the Albatross reaches the pirates' island, Peg Traherne swims ashore. As the pirates prepare to set out to sea, Peg hides in a tumbledown shack. Inside she is amazed to discover a collection of papers belonging to Obadiah Walrus. These include two pages from his diary and a plan of the pirates' base, the Fort of Skulls. Peg discovers that Obadiah managed to escape from the pirates, only to be recaptured during a bid to rescue ten fellow prisoners. Using the plan and the information in the diary, Peg can find a safe route to the prisoners' chamber.

The Statue of the God of Jests was made in Octana village

Persimmon Isle

Saskatoon Isle

Parana

As we neared the Heliotropic Isles, a bloodcurdling shout of "Pirates ahoy" rang out from the lookout's perch. Within minutes, the ship was swarming with ruffianly buccaneers, and we were fighting hand to hand upon the main deck. Yet hardly had the fighting begun than Lieutenant Draconio (who was in charge of the ship) ordered the crew to surrender! The pirates loaded their longboats with booty, taking with them the Calypso Figure. I could not contain my indignation, and lunged at the villains with my cutlass. Someone shouted "Look out, Mr Walrus!" but before I could react, I was in the clutches of a treacherous pirate.

The pirates took me to their fortress, but I bribed one of them to help me escape. He gave me a plan of the fort and released me from the Prisoners' Chamber.

The next day, however, I was determined to re-enter the fort so that I could release the other wretched captives. I waited until sunset, then slipped inside the fort through an unguarded entrance. I followed the corridor straight in front of me, then darted through the first door on my left whereupon I found myself in the Torture Chamber. I crept out through the same door and turned left into the corridor once more. I slipped through the first door on the right, and found myself in the Gunroom.

I continued to explore the fort, fearful at every moment lest I should collide with a fierce buccaneer, until I entered the pirates' Sleeping Quarters. I crossed

the room then opened a door which took me straight into a larger room which I identified as the Kitchens. At that moment I heard the shouts and oaths of approaching pirates, and hastily retreated. I cannot remember my route, but at last I took refuge in a large fireplace in the Granary. When I judged it safe to emerge, I returned to the corridor. This time, I turned right, then took the first door on the left, whereupon I entered the Banqueting Hall. After that I cannot remember my route, but I know that at some point I reached the Private Den of Buccaneer Bess, where all the pirates had assembled and were indulging in devilish merriment; and finally I reached the door of the Prisoners' Chamber, which is a smaller room.

At that moment, I was spotted by a fiery pirate, who came charging toward me, cutlass at the ready. I ran as fast as I could, dodging through the great fortress until I came to the Private Room of Barebones Jake. I crossed the room, burst through the door into a corridor, turned left and flung myself through the first door on the right. I was in the Gunpowder Room, which I knew concealed the entrance to a secret tunnel. Just as a group of pirates burst into the room, I found the tunnel entrance and made my escape.

Mercifully, in all my wanderings I managed to avoid the devilish booby traps of Buccaneer Bess.

All this took place yesterday. Today I shall try my luck once more but this is indeed a perilous mission and I know not if I will succeed.

Camwood Isle

Capulin Island

Lamotte Isle

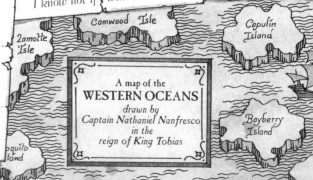

A map of the
WESTERN OCEANS
drawn by
Captain Nathaniel Nanfresco
in the
reign of King Tobias

...squito ...land

...Island

Bayberry Island

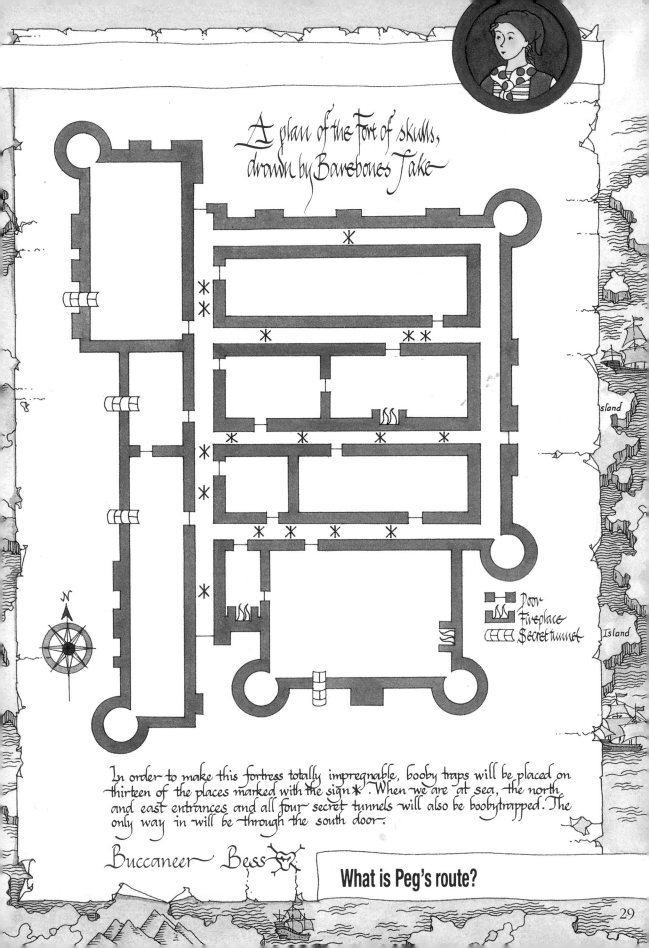

A plan of the Fort of skulls,
drawn by Barebones Jake

Island

Island

Door
Fireplace
Secret tunnel

N

In order to make this fortress totally impregnable, booby traps will be placed on thirteen of the places marked with the sign ✱. When we are at sea, the north and east entrances and all four secret tunnels will also be boobytrapped. The only way in will be through the south door.

Buccaneer Bess

What is Peg's route?

The Fair of Farrago

According to Aurora the Guardian of Secrets, the statue of the Cantador is hidden in the Amethyst Cave in the land of Magenta. The only person who knows the way to the cave is the Guardian's loyal pageboy, Blondel, who has gone to the Fair of Farrago on Magenta's border. The Guardian explains that Blondel will disguise himself as a different stallholder on each day of the fair.

This tapestry shows the Annual Fair of Farrago.
By the fair's ancient custom, each stall displays a flag and two shields. Each shield is divided into halves.
When the fair first began, each flag had a number and each shield had two numbers, one in each half. The numbers followed a rule. If the two numbers on the left-hand shield were multiplied together and the result was added to the sum of the two numbers on the right-hand shield, the result was the number on the flag.
As time passed, many of these numbers were lost and the number patterns were left incomplete.

Carilla must follow Blondel to the fair and identify each of his disguises. If she can find the pageboy on the last day of the fair, he will lead her to the Cantador's hiding place. This bright tapestry shows the stalls at the Fair of Farrago, together with all the information Carilla needs to reach the end of her quest.

On each of the five days of the fair, Blondel will be disguised as a different stallholder. He has chosen five stalls whose numbers form five sequences. The first sequence links the numbers in the top halves of the stalls' left-hand shields. The second links the numbers in the lower halves of these shields. The third links the numbers in the top halves of the right-hand shields. The fourth links the numbers in the lower halves of these shields. The numbers displayed on the flags of the five stalls form the final sequence. The number displayed on the flag of Blondel's first stall should be 17. The number on one of the shields on the final stall should be 13.

What are Blondel's disguises?

The Final Rendezvous

After recovering three of the stolen Faymus Treasures, Percival Sharpe arrives at the final handover point. Here he finds an envelope from his mysterious informer. Its contents reveal that the location of this handover has been changed in a last minute attempt to throw Percival off the trail.

April 28th

To Mr Sharpe,

I write to you in great haste. At the last minute the Cafelons have changed the arrangements for the handover of the final Treasure. I enclose copies of their revised instructions which have been sent to the thieves and their accomplices. Their contents should enable you to locate the new handover point.

Once you have recovered the treasure, do not pursue your investigations further. I am working undercover at the Cafelons headquarters and your inquiries could imperil my position.

Good Luck,

For the last time, your Informer

THE CANTADORA STEAMER

The Cantadora is the pride of the *Cadenza Shipping Line*. This elegant steamer boasts four luxurious passenger decks with three restaurants, two ballrooms, two sun decks and a casino. Among the members of the crew, we are pleased to number the Galliard Singers and M. Xavier Caviar, the world famous chef.

Top passenger deck

Second passenger deck

The Crystal Ballroom

ORDERS for A
You will go to the following places:
□ five minutes after boarding
✳ ten minutes after boarding
∽ fifteen minutes after boarding
ᴟ twenty minutes after boarding
ᴝ twenty five minutes after boarding

ORDERS for B
You will go to the following places:
✳ five minutes after boarding
∽ ten minutes after boarding
□ fifteen minutes after boarding
ᴟ twenty minutes after boarding
+ twenty five minutes after boarding

ORDERS for C
You will go to the following places:
∽ five minutes after boarding
✳ ten minutes after boarding
+ fifteen minutes after boarding
△ twenty minutes after boarding
φ twenty five minutes after boarding

According to the revised arrangements, the thieves will hand over the treasure to their accomplices during one of four meetings aboard the Cantadora steamer at the port of Cadenza. Percival must use information from his informer to discover exactly when and where this meeting will take place.

From the classical restraint of the *Crystal Ballroom* to the exuberant opulence of the *Imperial Restaurant*, every aspect of the Cantadora is finely crafted for the passenger's delight. Those who wish to experience the voyage of a lifetime are requested to write to Captain Draconio, c/o *Cadenza Shipping Line*, Cadenza.

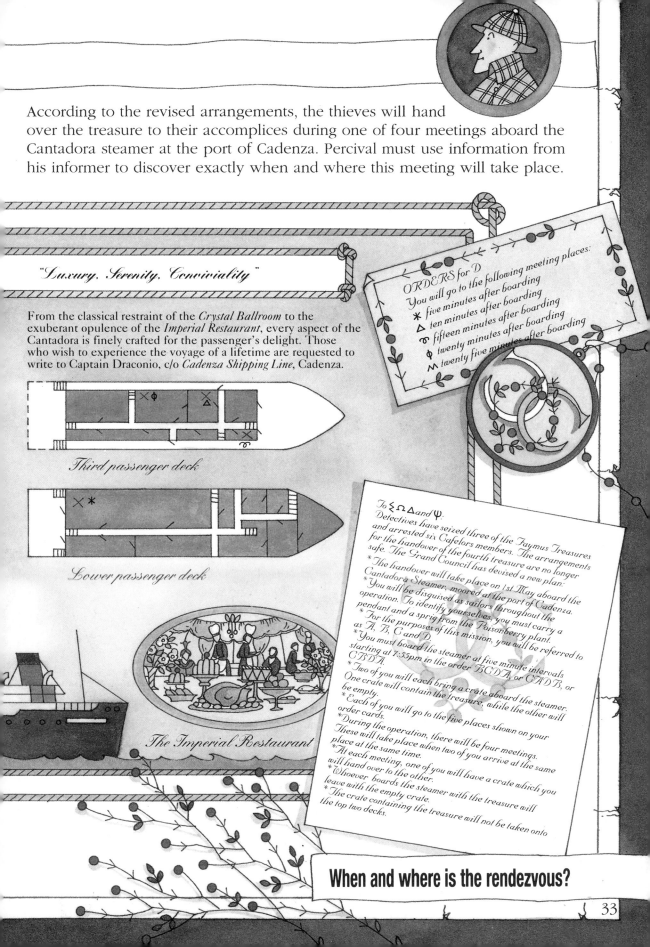

Third passenger deck

Lower passenger deck

The Imperial Restaurant

ORDERS for D
You will go to the following meeting places:
✴ five minutes after boarding
△ ten minutes after boarding
ઈ fifteen minutes after boarding
φ twenty minutes after boarding
⋈ twenty five minutes after boarding

To ξ Ω △ and Ψ:
Detectives have seized three of the Faymus Treasures and arrested six Cafelors members. The arrangements for the handover of the fourth treasure are no longer safe. The Grand Council has devised a new plan:
* The handover will take place on 1st May aboard the Cantadora Steamer, moored at the port of Cadenza.
* You will be disguised as sailors throughout the operation. To identify yourselves, you must carry a pendant and a sprig from the Poisonberry plant.
* For the purposes of this mission, you will be referred to as A, B, C and D.
* You must board the steamer at five minute intervals starting at 7.55pm in the order BCDA or CADB, or CBDA.
* Two of you will each bring a crate aboard the steamer. One crate will contain the treasure, while the other will be empty.
* Each of you will go to the five places shown on your order cards.
* During the operation, there will be four meetings. These will take place when two of you arrive at the same place at the same time.
* At each meeting, one of you will have a crate which you will hand over to the other.
* Whoever boards the steamer with the treasure will leave with the empty crate.
* The crate containing the treasure will not be taken onto the top two decks.

When and where is the rendezvous?

Treasure Hunt

Secret agent Peg Traherne releases Obadiah Walrus and ten fellow prisoners from the Fort of Skulls. Having found the leader of the Society of Alfresco, her mission is over, but her adventures are not yet at an end. Obadiah explains that he was taking a priceless statue called the Calypso Figure to a secret destination. Now this statue has fallen into the pirates' hands. It must be recovered at all costs and Obadiah needs Peg's help.

Four months ago, I struck a deal with a certain Lieutenant Draconio. Draconio, in temporary command of the Albatross, invited me to attack his ship and promised that the crew would put up only a show of a fight. He agreed to allow me to take five valuable treasures from the ship — but in return I was to hand over the treasure known as the Calypso Figure to members of a shadowy organization called the Cafelors.

The attack was a great success, but I took a liking to the Calypso Figure and resolved to keep it for myself. Before the Cafelors could claim the statue I decided to hide it in a secret place on the island of Cinnabar. While exploring this island, I identified nine possible hiding places. I laid booby traps at eight of these sites and buried the figure at the ninth place.

On my return to the Fort of Skulls, I devised a cunning treasure chart which shows all the nine places on Cinnabar, together with all the tracks that connect them. Each track links two places and passes through one camp. Where two places are joined like this ✳ it means that the path between them goes through camp ✳ and so on.

Each of the nine places has a symbol. The hiding place of the Calypso Figure has the symbol 📦

The track from X to ♘ goes through camp ✳ but only if the track from ♄ to ⚷ leads through camp ⊕

The track from ⚷ to ♄ goes through camp ☉ but only if the track from ♅ to ♘ leads through camp △

The track from hiding place ⚓ to hiding place ♡ goes through camp ☉

The track from ♈ to ♡ leads through camp ✳ but only if the route from ⚷ to ⚓ leads through camp △

The track from hiding place ♈ to hiding place ⚷ goes through camp ◇

The track from ♘ to ♅ goes through camp ⊕ but only if the track from X to 📦 leads through camp ✳

The track from hiding place ♡ to hiding place X goes through camp +

The track from X to ♘ goes through camp ⊕ but only if the track from ♄ to ♈ leads through camp ☉

The Calypso Figure →

While searching the fort, Peg and Obadiah find a secret notebook belonging to the pirate captain. From its contents they learn that the Calypso Figure has been hidden on the island of Cinnabar. The duo must make sense of an ingenious treasure chart to discover which of this island's numerous hiding places conceals the statue. They must search in the right place, or else they will fall foul of the pirates' deadly booby traps.

Where is the Calypso Figure?

The Raider's Fort

The search for the Weather Charm of Wailen Valla leads Skarpa the Bold across the Isle of Doom Laiden to the grim fort of the raider of Maelstrom. On his way, he meets three prisoners who have escaped from the fort. The trio tell Skarpa that the Weather Charm is hidden in a small chest in the raider's treasure chamber. They present him with six clay tablets and a plan of the fort. With these, Skarpa must first locate the treasure chamber then find a safe route to it, retrieve the stolen charm and return to safety.

PATROL 1

PATROL 2

PATROL 3

PATROL 4

PATROL 5

PATROL 6

THE FORT CAN BE ENTERED THROUGH A
TUNNEL WHICH LEADS INTO THE BREWERY.
BE WARNED: SIX GUARDS PATROL THE FORT
DURING THE NIGHT. THE CLAY TABLETS
SHOW THE ROOMS ON THEIR PATROL ROUTES,
IN THE ORDER THEY ARE VISITED. THE
GUARDS GO DIRECTLY FROM ROOM TO ROOM.
EACH ROOM HAS A DIFFERENT SYMBOL:

SLEEPING QUARTERS –
TREASURE CHAMBER –
KITCHENS –
GUARDSROOM –
BANQUETING HALL –
GRANARY –
HALL OF AXENSORD –
BAKERY –
HALL OF GRENDAL –
BREWERY –

FROM THE CLAY TABLETS YOU CAN
DISCOVER WHICH ROOMS LIE NEXT TO ONE
ANOTHER AND NAME THE TEN ROOMS
SHOWN ON THE PLAN. THEN YOU CAN MAKE
YOUR WAY TO THE TREASURE CHAMBER –
BUT BIDE YOUR TIME.
YOU MAY ONLY ENTER ROOMS NOT ON THE
PATROL ROUTE OF THE CURRENT GUARD. IF
YOU ENTER A ROOM ON THE ROUTE OF THE
NEXT GUARD, YOU MUST LEAVE THAT ROOM
BEFORE HIS PATROL BEGINS.
A BELL RINGS OUT EVERY HOUR TO MARK
THE CHANGE OF GUARD.
BY STEALTHILY CREEPING FROM ONE SAFE
ROOM TO ANOTHER, AND WAITING FOR THE
CHANGE OF GUARD, YOU WILL BE ABLE TO
REACH THE TREASURE CHAMBER AND
RETURN TO THE BREWERY TO MAKE
YOUR ESCAPE.
TAKE THE TALISMAN WITH YOU. IT SHOWS
THE WEATHER CHARM AND WILL BRING YOU
GOOD LUCK.

THE STATUE OF THE GOD OF POETRY WAS MADE IN MANZANA VILLAGE

What is Skarpa's route?

The Enigma of the Palace

The trail of the Alfrescan Casket leads Freya de Fresque to a ruined palace high on the plains of Enkantador. On her way she retrieves a small package. This contains a letter and an old painting showing the palace during the reign of King Samerkand. Freya must use the painting to locate the palace's Chamber of Gold and Rubies, for this is where the casket lies hidden.

To the Seeker of the Alfrescan Casket,

The casket is inside the ruined palace on the Plains of Enkantador. It is hidden in a niche above the window of the Chamber of Gold and Rubies. To locate this room, you must use this painting which shows the palace during a visit by the Society of Alfresco eighty years ago.

+ Three of the visitors are on the roof of the palace while one of the rooms below one of the other six visitors is shown with a Magentan courtier. Each pair is engaged in a different activity.

+ The names of the visitors are Kappa, Iota, Tau, Gamma, Lambda, Bala, Omega, Zara and Theta.

+ Piece together the information on the right-hand side of the painting to discover which of the rooms is the Chamber of Gold and Rubies.

Good luck, and may the casket restore hope and good fortune to Alfresco.

Reading

Bathing

Music

The ruined palace

The nine members of the Society of Alfresco were entertained by King Samerkand the Wise. On the fourth day of their visit, the king invited the Alfrescans to his palace on the Plains of Enkantador. This painting shows the king on the palace roof with three of the visitors together with his Chief Falconer and the Court Artist.
Kappa is not in the same room as the Grand Vizier or the Snake Charmer.
The Conjuror is not feasting.
Tau is being entertained by the Acrobat.
Neither the Acrobat nor the Conjurer are in the Dragon Room.
The people in the Chamber of the Djinni are not bathing, playing chess, or feasting.
Lambda is not in the Chamber of Gold and Rubies, nor in the Peacock room. Bala is not in the same room as the Poet or the Chief of Ceremonies.

Neither the Poet, nor the Chief of Ceremonies, nor the Snake Charmer are reading.
The Poet is not in the Chamber of the Djinni.
Kappa is playing chess. The people in the Peacock Room are either feasting or playing music.
Lambda is not in the same room as the Grand Vizier.
Neither the Grand Vizier nor the Snake Charmer are bathing.
Bala is not in the Zebek Room or the Peacock Room.
Neither Kappa nor Iota is in the Dragon Room.
The Grand Vizier is not in the Zebek Room.
The people in the Zebek Room are not feasting.
Gamma is not in the same room as the Chief of Ceremonies.
Iota is not playing music.
Lambda is not dancing, bathing, or playing music.
Neither the Chief of Ceremonies, nor the Grand Vizier, nor the Snake Charmer are dancing.
The Conjuror is not in the Chamber of the Djinni or the Zebek Room. The people in the Dragon Room are not feasting, reading, or playing music.
The Snake Charmer is not in the Chamber of the Five Hundred Candles, the Chamber of the Djinni, or the Peacock Room.

Which is the Chamber of Gold and Rubies?

The Game of Alfresco

The final search for the statues of Alfresco begins when Freya de Fresque retrieves the Alfrescan Casket. The seven ancient statues were stolen by the villainous Cafelors during the Dismal Age of Turmoil and Strife. One of them was later found by Skarpa the Bold and another by Carilla di Galliard, but sadly both were lost again. During the Swashbuckling Age of Buccaneers, the Society of Alfresco was formed to track down the statues and return

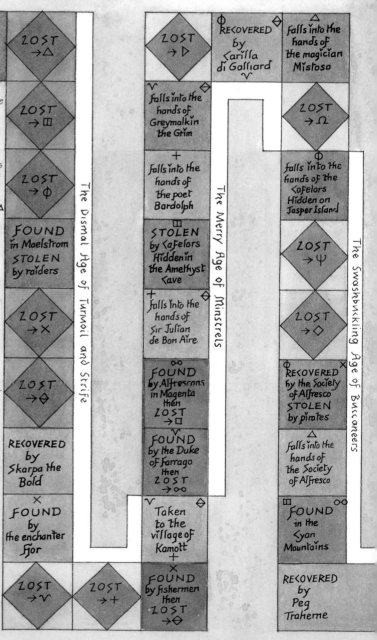

START
At the dawn of the Dismal Age of Turmoil and Strife, the statues are stolen by the Cafelors

The Game of Alfresco
Each of the seven pieces in this game represents one of the statues of Alfresco.

At each turn, the players throw two dice and move their pieces around the board according to the number they throw. If a player throws a double, he or she has an extra throw.

Instructions are written on some of the squares. Where the symbols →△ appear, the player must move his or her piece to any of the squares marked with the symbol △. If the symbols →□ appear, the piece must be moved to a square marked □ and so on. The player has to decide which square to choose.

This is a special version of the game, designed to reveal the hiding place of the real statues. There are four extra rules in this version:

1. Only one piece may land on each square in the course of the game.
2. Sometimes a piece may land on more than one square during a turn. This happens if the player throws a double or if the piece lands on a LOST square. For example, a piece might land on a square marked LOST → Ψ and then move on to another square marked Ψ. If this happens, neither of these two squares can be used again during the game.
3. However, all the pieces must finish on the same square. Once you have identified this square, you will know where the statues lie hidden.
4. The pieces follow a special set of moves which match their histories. For example, the statue of the God of Music was hidden in the Amethyst Cave then recovered by Carilla di Galliard. The piece representing this statue must therefore pass through the two squares that mention these events. You will need to know two or three important events in the histories of the statues depicting the gods of food, dance and poetry.

FOOD

MUSIC

JESTS

ACROBATICS

them to the island. Over the next two centuries its members recovered all seven. However, before the society could return them to the island, the Cafelors blockaded its shores. The statues were hidden by the society and cryptic clues to their location were left inside the Alfrescan Casket. Now the Cafelors have left Alfresco, but no one can make sense of the casket's contents and so find the seven statues.

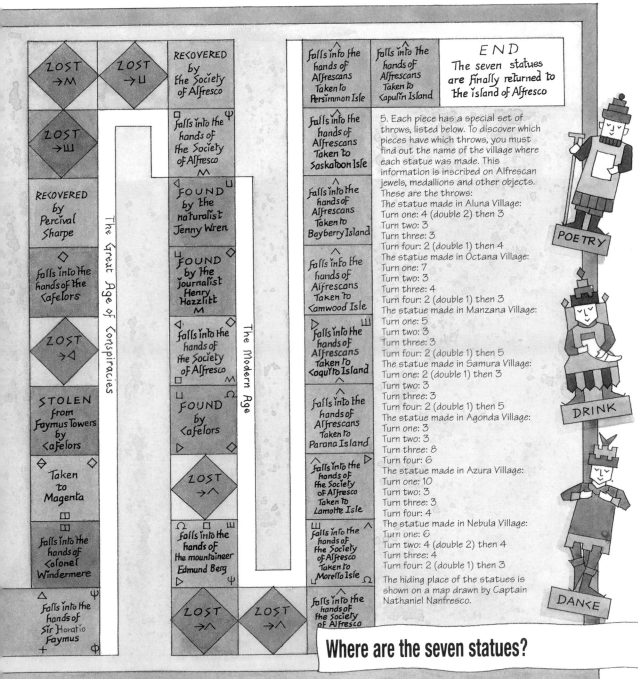

LOST →M

LOST →Ⅱ

RECOVERED by the Society of Alfresco

falls into the hands of Alfrescans Taken to Persimmon Isle

falls into the hands of Alfrescans Taken to Capulin Island

END
The seven statues are finally returned to the island of Alfresco

LOST →Ⅲ

falls into the hands of the Society of Alfresco M

falls into the hands of Alfrescans Taken to Saskatoon Isle

RECOVERED by Percival Sharpe

FOUND by the naturalist Jenny Wren

falls into the hands of Alfrescans Taken to Bayberry Island

The Great Age of Conspiracies

The Modern Age

5. Each piece has a special set of throws, listed below. To discover which pieces have which throws, you must find out the name of the village where each statue was made. This information is inscribed on Alfrescan jewels, medallions and other objects. These are the throws:

The statue made in Aluna Village:
Turn one: 4 (double 2) then 3
Turn two: 3
Turn three: 3
Turn four: 2 (double 1) then 4

The statue made in Octana Village:
Turn one: 7
Turn two: 3
Turn three: 4
Turn four: 2 (double 1) then 3

The statue made in Manzana Village:
Turn one: 5
Turn two: 3
Turn three: 3
Turn four: 2 (double 1) then 5

The statue made in Samura Village:
Turn one: 2 (double 1) then 3
Turn two: 3
Turn three: 3
Turn four: 2 (double 1) then 5

The statue made in Agonda Village:
Turn one: 3
Turn two: 3
Turn three: 8
Turn four: 6

The statue made in Azura Village:
Turn one: 10
Turn two: 3
Turn three: 3
Turn four: 4

The statue made in Nebula Village:
Turn one: 6
Turn two: 4 (double 2) then 4
Turn three: 4
Turn four: 2 (double 1) then 3

The hiding place of the statues is shown on a map drawn by Captain Nathaniel Nanfresco.

falls into the hands of Alfrescans Taken to Camwood Isle

FOUND by the journalist Henry Hazzlitt M

falls into the hands of the Society of Alfresco

falls into the hands of Alfrescans Taken to Coquito Island

falls into the hands of Alfrescans Taken to Parana Island

STOLEN from Faymus Towers by Cafelors

FOUND by Cafelors

falls into the hands of the Society of Alfresco Taken to Lamotte Isle

Taken to Magenta

LOST →∧

falls into the hands of Colonel Windermere

falls into the hands of the mountaineer Edmund Berg

falls into the hands of the Society of Alfresco Taken to Morello Isle

falls into the hands of Sir Horatio Faymus

LOST →∧

LOST →∧

falls into the hands of the Society of Alfresco

POETRY

DRINK

DANCE

Where are the seven statues?

Clues

Page 4

(1) The easiest way to solve this puzzle is to use a special grid. Here is a simplified version of the puzzle to explain how the grid works. Three characters – Shark, Jonson and Graves – are guarding three entrances of Castle Cloud – the East Tower, the Bell Tower and the North Tower. Each guard is known by a different symbol. One guard is Ψ, another is Ω and the third is Σ.

Shark guards the Bell Tower and is not Ψ. Graves is not Σ. Ψ does not guard the East Tower. Σ does not guard the Bell Tower. Which tower does Jonson guard?

To solve the puzzle, first of all, draw a grid as shown below. Where you know that two things go together, put a tick in the relevant box on the grid. Where you know that two things do not go together, put a cross. With all the information entered, the grid should look like this:

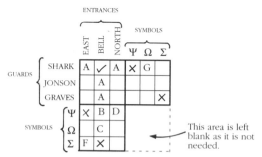

Since Shark guards the Bell Tower, he does not guard the East Tower or the North Tower; and neither Jonson nor Graves guards the Bell Tower, so you can add crosses to the grid in the boxes marked A. You know that Shark guards the Bell Tower and is not Ψ. Therefore the Bell Tower is not guarded by Ψ, so you can put a cross in box B. Since the Bell Tower is not guarded by Σ either, it must be guarded by Ω – put a tick in box C.

Ψ does not guard the Bell Tower and does not guard the East Tower either, so he guards the North Tower – put a tick in box D. In turn, this means that Σ guards the East Tower – put a tick in box F.

The Bell Tower is guarded by Ω and by Shark, so Shark is Ω – put a tick in box G. Can you identify Jonson's symbol? What about Graves's? Your grid should now look like this:

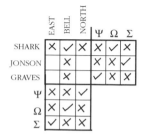

Finally, Ψ guards the North Tower and is Graves, so Graves guards the North Tower. Now you should be able to identify Jonson's Tower.

(2) To solve the puzzle on page 4, you will need to draw a larger grid as there are seven guards, seven entrances and seven symbols. Draw the grid and enter all the information. Remember that Hook guards the South

Tower or the Ghost Tower and is either ⋏ or Ә or ∇ or Ω. Neither the South Tower nor the Ghost Tower is guarded by Ә ∇ or Ω, so Hook is not Ә ∇ or Ω. Therefore, by a process of elimination, Hook is ⋏. Now can you identify Clipper's sign? Next identify Jonson's sign, remembering that he guards either the East Tower or the Old Keep.

Page 5

If Skarpa chose the symbol representing the Vale of Tor in the fourth column, this would exclude all three symbols in the second column, so this symbol must be wrong. What would happen if he chose the Fjord of Eirik in the third column? And what about the Lake of Frija in the second column?

Page 6

(1) First translate the symbols on the emblems into numbers, then piece together the five sequences.

(2) Now discover how the shapes move. Look at the first two emblems. The circle goes from top left to bottom right. The square goes from bottom right to top right. Where do the other shapes move to? Does the symbol in the top left section always move to the bottom right section in the following emblem? Does the symbol in the bottom right section always move to the top right section?

Page 7

(1) Identify the mummer who always tells the truth. Could it be the drummer? (Think carefully about his statement, "I always tell a mixtue of truth and lies"). Could it be the piper? If it is neither, could it be the juggler? (Look for contradictions in her statements.) What about the jester?

(2) Now identify the mummer who always lies. Could it be the juggler? If not, when does the juggler tell the truth? Does this help you find the liar?

(3) Next think very carefully about the drummer's first statement. Is it true or false? If it is false, what does he really say when asked how to find the statue? Would this be true or false? Which road should Carilla take?

(4) How many of the jester's statements are correct?

Pages 8-9

(1) Start with the Forest of Tyre. Could it either of the forests in the middle row? (Remember that the Forest of Tyre is over five days' walk from Lapis Lazuli and from one of the three lakes). Now can you identify Lake Tirin?

(2) Lake Aral must be one of the two remaining lakes Knowing this, can you rule out one possibility for the Djinni Mountains? Could the Djinni Mountains be in the middle row? Now can you identify Lake Aral?

Pages 10-11

(1) Start by numbering the islands from one to six (it does not matter which island has which number). Then draw a chart like this:

FLAGS:	1 ⊓	2 ▷	3 ◁	4 ⋈	5 ◣	6 ◤
ISLAND 1	A					
ISLAND 2						
etc						

(2) In each box, write in the four symbols for the relevant village. For instance, in the box marked A, write in the symbols shown for the village on island 1 with flag 1. Now look at the symbols for the villages with flag 4. How many villages have symbol 𝍫? If it is only one,

then ⊞ must be the correct symbol for this village. In turn this means that no other village on the same island has symbol ⊞

Pages 12-13

(1) First label the knights (K1, K2, K3 etc) then label the shields (S1, S2 etc) and the horses (H1, H2 etc).
(2) Now draw a grid as explained in the clue for page 4. Down the side, write the names of the ten knights (Gawain, Fernando, etc), then the horses' numbers (H1 to H10), then the knights' numbers (K1 to K10). Across the top, write in the shields' numbers (S1 to S10), then the knights' numbers, then the horses' numbers.
(3) Remember that if, for instance, K2 is holding S5, then you can put a tick in the K2/S5 box.

Pages 14-15

(1) Draw a grid as explained in the clue for page 4. Down the side of the grid, write the names of the five officers, followed by the ship's supplies, and then the decks. Across the top of the grid, write the names of the five treasures, then the decks, then the ship's supplies.
(2) The Casket of Magenta is not on Kraken's deck, and it is on the Gun Deck. Neither Bosun nor Windlass commands the Gun Deck, so the Casket of Magenta is either on Draconio's or Skurvy's deck. Neither Draconio nor Skurvy commands the deck where the spare sails are stored, so the Casket of Magenta is not on the same deck as the spare sails. Could the Casket of Magenta be on the same deck as the firearms? If not, what does this tell you?

Pages 16-17

(1) Use a grid as explained in the clue for page 4. Down the side of the grid, write the names of the members of the Dodo Club, then the dates on which they left Cragge, then the five means of transport. Across the top, write the names of the guests, then the means of transport, then the dates of departure.
(2) Remember that if Charlie Bounder left three days before Priscilla Prince, this means that Bounder did not leave on the 5th or 7th; and that Priscilla Prince did not leave on the 1st or 2nd.
(3) Spratt arrived at Marshby three days after Johnson. We know that Spratt went by train. If Johnson also went by train, he left three days before Spratt. If Johnson went by road, he left four days before Spratt.
(4) Once you have completed the grid, read the end of Percival's diary entry and the first item on the news cutting to identify the thieves.

Page 18

(1) Start by drawing a diagram of the pavilions like this:

RED FLAG		
POSITION 1	POSITION 2	POSITION 3
POSITION 4	POSITION 5	

YELLOW FLAG		
POSITION 6		POSITION 7
POSITION 8	POSITION 9	POSITION 10

(2) In each of the ten positions, write the first letter of the ten musicians' names. If a musician cannot be in a particular position, cross out the relevant letter.
(3) Which positions could Qat and Korabeth occupy? What about Lalik and Izarin – each has only six possible positions.
(4) Three pairs of musicians are next to one another. Two other musicians (Aramis and Faron) are in the same pavilion but not next to one another. With this in mind, can Korabeth be in position 9? Can Qat be in position 9?
(5) If Aramis and Faron were in the pavilion with the yellow flag, either they would occupy positions 8 and 10, or one would be in the front row and the other in the back row. Remembering that Qat is in the front row of one or other pavilion, and that three pairs of musicians sit next to one another, could Aramis and Faron be in the pavilion with the yellow flag? Next, discover which pavilion Izarin, Lalik, Haliah and Raban occupy.
(6) Which pavilion does Qat occupy? Can you narrow down the possible positions for Sulah and Balbek – remember they are next to one another. What would happen if Aramis or Faron was in position 2? Next, does Lalik have a cloak? What does this tell you about Aramis? Can Korabeth be in positions 6 or 7? If not, does he have a white turban?

Page 19

Draw a grid, as explained in the clue for page 4. Across the top, write the names of the islands, followed by the landmarks (volcano, hermitage etc). Down the side of the grid, write the names of the different Runaatongs, then the landmarks.

Pages 20-21

Use a grid, as explained in the clue for page 4. Down the side of the grid write the names of the places raided by the Whirlwind, then the years, then the warlords. Across the top, write the names of the forts, then the warlords, then the years.

Pages 22-23

(1) The Tower of Four Winds is across the river from the Tower of Torment, but only if the Tower of Four Winds has a pointed doorway. Assume that the Tower of Four Winds does have a pointed doorway. What are the possible positions for the Tower of Torment? What if the Tower of Four Winds does not have a pointed doorway?
(2) The Tower of Belle is across the river from the Tower of Torment – what are its possible positions? Find another clue that will tell you which position is correct. Next, what would happen if the Tower of Rigadoon was on a hilltop? Once you have tried this out, you should have just three possible positions for this tower. Can you reduce the possible positions for the Tower of Rooks to two?

Pages 24-25

(1) Use a grid as explained in the clue for page 4. Down the side, write the names of the treasures, then the four months, then the symbols and then the handover points. Across the top, write the names of the cities, then the handover points, then the symbols, and then the months.
(2) The handover in Ehrhardt is two months before the one in Kastler. Therefore the handover in Ehrhardt is not in March or April, and the one in Kastler is not in January or February. Refer back to this clue (and others like it) as you solve the puzzle.

Pages 26-27

(1) How many possible routes are there for the Tri?
(2) Remembering that only one piece can land on each square in the course of the game, what are the possible routes for the other three pieces? The Rond has two, the Lo-Zeng has four and the Karray has eight.
(3) What would happen if the Karray used square D12? What about E3? Which piece uses square C7?

Pages 28-29

(1) What does Obadiah's diary tell you about the Granary, the Kitchens and the Sleeping Quarters? Each has only three possible positions. What are they?
(2) Which rooms on the plan can be the Gunpowder Room? How does Obadiah get to the Torture Chamber?

Using this information, can you find just three possible positions for this room?

(3) Now look at the way the rooms are linked together. For instance, if the Granary was in the southeast corner of the fort, where would the Banqueting Hall be?

(4) Putting everything together, can you find six different ways of labelling the rooms in the fort?

(5) Now read Buccaneer Bess's note on the plan. Remembering that Obadiah avoided the pirates' booby-traps, which of the six combinations is correct?

Pages 30-31

Fill in the gaps on the stalls where only one number is missing. Now draw a chart. At the top, write out the numbers on the flags, from the smallest to the largest. Beneath each flag number, write out the shield numbers (where you know them) for the relevant stall. Now look for possible patterns in the shield numbers. You should find two or three incomplete sequences for each position. Blondel's final stall has the number 13, so one sequence must end with this number. Does this help you identify the correct sequences?

Pages 32-33

(1) Start by drawing a chart, as indicated here:

	Boarding order 1				Boarding order 2				Boarding order 3			
TIME	B	C	D	A		C	A	D	B		C	B	D	A
7:55													
8:00	✳												
8:05	♈												
ETC													

(2) Looking at the cards, you can see that if B was the first to board, he would be at point ✳ at 8:00 (five minutes after boarding), at point ♈ at 8:05 and so on. Add this information to the chart (it has been started for you), then do the same for the other Cafelors members. Next do the same for the other boarding orders.

(3) A meeting takes place when two Cafelors are in the same place at the same time. Where would the meetings be if the villains boarded in order 1? Who would be involved? What about orders 2 and 3? (Two meetings can take place at the same time.)

(4) There are two crates, and one crate is to be handed over at each meeting. At the first meeting, there are four possible scenarios. If the meeting is between A and D, then either A hands the crate with the treasure to D; or D hands this crate to A; or A hands the empty crate to D; or D hands the empty crate to A.

Assume that D hands the empty crate to A at the first meeting, and that the second meeting is between C and D. At this meeting, C must hand the crate with the treasure to D. If the meeting is between C and A, A would hand the empty crate to C. Using similar reasoning, figure out all the scenarios for the different boarding orders.

(5) Remember that the person who boards with the treasure will leave with the empty crate.

(6) Finally, figure out which decks the genuine crate would be taken to in each possibility. Remember to include the places the crate is taken to between meetings.

Pages 34-35

(1) Draw a chart to show the routes between the different hiding places as indicated here.

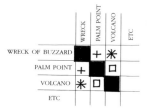

(2) Draw a grid with the names of the hiding places down the side, and their symbols along the top. If you discover, for instance, that ⚑ is not the Devil's Cave, put a cross in the relevant box. If you discover that ⚑ is the Devil's Cave, put a tick in that box.

(3) The track from ⚐ to ✗ goes through +. Look at the chart. How many hiding places are joined by a track going through + ? The track from ♄ to ⚐ goes through ☊. You should have only two possibilities for ⚐. What are the possibilities for ♄?

(4) The track from ♈ to ⚐ goes through ✳ but only if the track from ♋ to ♄ goes through △ . ♄ has two possibilities; ♋ has seven. With these possibilities in mind, can the track from ♄ to ♋ go through ✳ ?

Pages 36-37

(1) From the clay tablets, you know that, for instance, a door leads from ⚒ into ◈ ⬆ 7 and ☒ . ⚒ must therefore have at least four doors. Draw a chart showing each room, its minimum number of doors and which rooms it is next to.

(2) There is one room in the fort with only one door. This has to be either ✳ or 7. What would happen if it was 7?

(3) Once you have identified the room with one door, you can easily identify the room next to it. Now what do you know about the positions of ⚛ ⚛ ⬆ and ◈? And what about ⚒ ⊡ 7 and ✗ ? Next identify the room with two doors. There are now only two possibilities. Which is correct? Having identified all ten rooms, look at the clay tablets again. Which rooms are safe during each patrol?

Pages 38-39

(1) Draw a grid as described in the clue for page 4. Down the side write the names of the guests, then the names of the courtiers, then the rooms. Across the top, write the activities, then the rooms, then the courtiers.

(2) Lambda is either reading or feasting. Assume that he is feasting. Is this possible? Once you know, find out which courtier is reading, then which activity is taking place in the Chamber of the Five Hundred Candles. You should now know that either the poet or the acrobat is dancing. Assume that it is the poet. Is this possible?

Pages 40-41

To find out which set of throws belongs to each piece, look back through the book to discover where each statue was made. Each piece follows a set of moves that matches its history. Which two squares must the god of poetry use? (The statue may have more than one name – look at page 37.) Which two squares must the god of dance use? (Again, the statue has more than one name – look at pages 19 and 34.) Can you find three squares for the god of food? (For its other name, look at page 25.) Now you are ready to start playing the game. Start by numbering the squares from 1 to 60. Then write out all the possible routes for each piece, remembering that if, for instance, square 21 is used by the piece representing the god of music, it cannot be used by any other piece. Some pieces have more than fifteen routes! Next, decide which piece uses square 33. Then look at 13, 19, 18, 14, 48, 32 and 15 in turn. Now what are the possible end squares? (There should be three.) Try each in turn - which is correct?

Answers

Page 4

From the letter, Peg knows that the safe entrance is the one guarded by Morgrim.
Piecing together the information supplied by the Society of Alfresco, she makes the following discoveries:

Shark is Ø and guards the South Tower
Smythe is ⋛ and guards the Old Keep
Hook is ⋏ and guards the Ghost Tower

Graves is ∇ and guards the North Tower
Clipper is Ə and guards the Bell Tower
Jonson is Ω and guards the East Tower
Morgrim is Ψ and guards the Great Hall

Peg should therefore use the entrance to the Great Hall.

Page 5

Skarpa should choose the symbols ringed here:

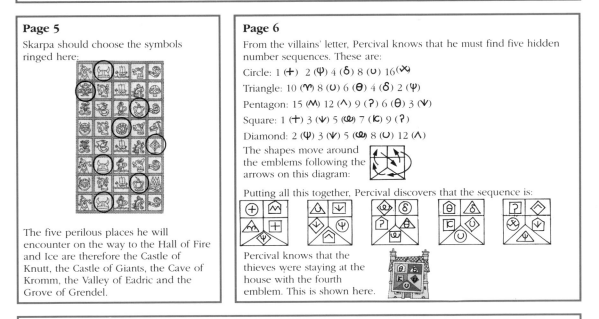

The five perilous places he will encounter on the way to the Hall of Fire and Ice are therefore the Castle of Knutt, the Castle of Giants, the Cave of Kromm, the Valley of Eadric and the Grove of Grendel.

Page 6

From the villains' letter, Percival knows that he must find five hidden number sequences. These are:

Circle: 1 (+) 2 (Ψ) 4 (δ) 8 (∪) 16 (✕)

Triangle: 10 (⋔) 8 (∪) 6 (θ) 4 (δ) 2 (Ψ)

Pentagon: 15 (⋔) 12 (∧) 9 (?) 6 (θ) 3 (∨)

Square: 1 (+) 3 (∨) 5 (⚌) 7 (𝐊) 9 (?)

Diamond: 2 (Ψ) 3 (∨) 5 (⚌) 8 (∪) 12 (∧)

The shapes move around the emblems following the arrows on this diagram:

Putting all this together, Percival discovers that the sequence is:

Percival knows that the thieves were staying at the house with the fourth emblem. This is shown here.

Page 7

Carilla deduces that the bear always tells the truth, the drummer always lies and the other mummers tell a mixture of truth and lies. To discover which road to take, Carilla has to think very carefully about the drummer's first statement. The drummer always lies, so the statement is false. This means that if Carilla asked him directly which road she should take to find the statue, he would NOT reply, "You must take the road to the town of Tabor". He would actually reply, "You must take the road to Mandolin". This would itself be a lie, so Carilla must head for Tabor. Carilla must therefore head for Tabor; at the crossroads she should go to the Castle of Arc, where she should find the cook.

Pages 8-9

The names of the forests, lakes and mountains are shown here. Freya's route is marked in black.

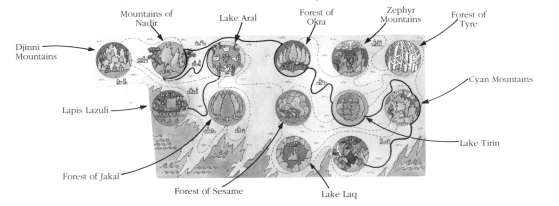

Pages 10-11

This is the village of Kamott

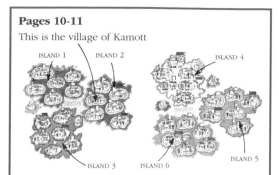

ISLAND 1 ISLAND 2 ISLAND 4
ISLAND 3 ISLAND 6 ISLAND 5

The following chart shows the secret signs of all the villages in the Runik Isles:

FLAGS:	1	2	3	4	5	6
ISLAND 1						
ISLAND 2						
ISLAND 3						
ISLAND 4						
ISLAND 5						
ISLAND 6						

Pages 12-13

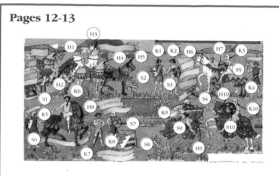

Piecing all the information together, Carilla can name all ten knights and identify their horses and shields:
Sir Gerard is K2. His horse is H4 and his shield is S3
Sir Fernando is K3. His horse is H7 and his shield is S5
Sir Caspar is K8. His horse is H1 and his shield is S7
Sir Almeric is K6. His horse is H8 and his shield is S1
Sir Emilio is K5. His horse is H6 and his shield is S6
Sir Harold is K4. His horse is H2 and his shield is S8
Sir Gawain is K7. His horse is H3 and his shield is S4
Sir Balthus is K10. His horse is H10 and his shield is S10
Sir Sigismund is K1. His horse is H5 and his shield is S2
Sir Jules is K9. His horse is H9 and his shield is S9

Pages 14-15

To identify Draconio's deck, Peg pieces together all the information on the plan of the ship. This is what she discovers:
Kraken commands the Lower Deck, where the Goldenhall Talisman and the spare sails are stored.
Skurvy commands the Gun Deck, where the Casket of Magenta and the ropes are stored.
Bosun commands the Quarterdeck, where the Tamarind Jewels and the ship's biscuits are stored.
Windlass commands the Poop Deck, where the Galliard Lute and the rum are stored.
Draconio commands the Main Deck, where the Calypso Figure and the firearms are stored.
Therefore the missing logbook is hidden on the Main Deck.

Pages 16-17

From the scattered pieces of information, Percival comes to the following conclusions:
Robert Johnson left Cragge with Jonathon Sutch by stagecoach on the 1st, arriving in Marshby on the 3rd.
Charlie Bounder left Cragge with Maria Jones on the Piston Express on the 2nd, arriving in Marshby on the 3rd.
The Marchioness of Rotunda left Cragge with Denholm Hazzlitt by carriage on the 4th, arriving in Marshby on the 6th.
Jacob Spratt left Cragge with Priscilla Prince on the Gantry Express on the 5th, arriving in Marshby on the 6th.
Lucinda Eliot left Cragge with Fanny Wren by hansom on the 7th, arriving in Marshby on the 9th.
Percival knows that the thieves, a man and a woman, stayed at the Swan Inn in Marshby. According to the newscutting, the inn was closed from January 6th to January 8th. The only man and woman to arrive in Marshby together when the inn was open are Charlie Bounder and Maria Jones. They must therefore be the thieves.

Page 18

Freya knows that she must go to the village of the musician, Aramis. Piecing together the information at the top of the painting, she is able to name all the musicians:

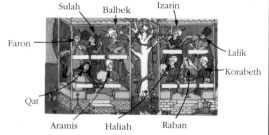

Sulah Balbek Izarin
Faron
Lalik
Korabeth
Qat
Aramis Haliah Raban

The names of the musicians' villages are written on their music stands. Aramis's village is Turmeric. This is where Freya should go next.

Page 19

From the "Wanted" poster, Peg knows that the pirates live in a fort built on the ruins of an ancient palace. To locate this palace, she has to piece together all the information in the documents. This is what she discovers: the Rufus Runaatong and the mango groves are on Jaspar Island; the Long-Tailed Runaatong and the swamps are on Eastern Island; the Klamorus Runaatong and the standing stones are on Corallina Island; the Short-Haired Runaatong and the hermitage are on Salamander Isle; the Howling Runaatong and the tower are on the Isle of Parakeets; the Silver-Haired Runaatong and the volcano are on Solferino Island; the Bouncing Runaatong and the ancient palace are on Cinnabar Island.

Therefore the pirates are based on Cinnabar Island.

Pages 20-21

To discover which fort he should search, Skarpa must first name the warlord who raided Maelstrom. From the information on the stone, Skarpa makes the following discoveries:

Erik the Mighty raided Vidar in the Year of the Storms. He lives in the Fort of High Towers.

Harold the Hardy raided Alfresco in the Year of the Mighty Seamonster. He lives in the North Fort.

Gunhilde the Ruthless raided Lilla Vaga in the Year of the Great Curse. She lives in the South Fort.

Sombrik the Proud raided Loki in the Year of the Midnight Sun. He lives in the Fort of Blackstone.

Knutt the Fearsome raided Maelstrom in the Year of the Heroic Sea Voyage. He lives in the Fort of the Dragonstone.

Skarpa should therefore search the Fort of the Dragonstone.

Pages 22-23

This is the Tower of the Guardian

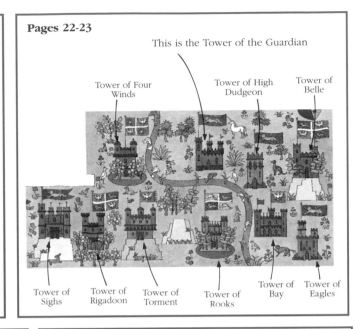

Tower of Four Winds

Tower of High Dudgeon

Tower of Belle

Tower of Sighs

Tower of Rigadoon

Tower of Torment

Tower of Rooks

Tower of Bay

Tower of Eagles

Pages 24-25

From the informer's notes, Percival can deduce exactly what the villains are planning to do:

In January, the Corsair's Toothpicks (♡) will be taken to Hotel Aurora in Bodoni

In February, the Galliard Lute (◊) will be taken to Marcato Mansion in Ehrhardt

In March, the Skarpa Talisman ( ) will be taken to the Great Arch of Grandioso in San Serif

In April, the Epicurean Idol ( ) will be taken to the Lady Aurora Steamer in Kastler

Pages 26-27

To locate the hiding place of the Alfrescan Casket, Freya must figure out the moves of the four pieces in the special version of Kaballo. The moves are as follows:

Tri:	A3	C5	E7	C9	E11
Rond:	A13	D12	G11	H8	I5
Lo-Zeng:	A4	D2	B5	E3	B1
Karray:	A6	B4	D5	C7	B9

Following the instructions in the letter, Freya therefore draws one line from B9 to I5 and another from B1 to E11. The lines cross in square D8, which shows a palace. This is where the Alfrescan Casket is hidden.

Pages 28-29

Peg's route to the Prisoners' Chamber is shown in black.

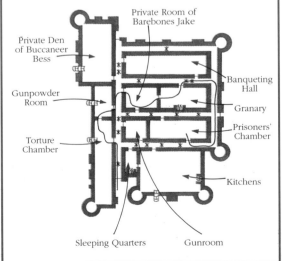

Private Room of Barebones Jake

Private Den of Buccaneer Bess

Gunpowder Room

Banqueting Hall

Granary

Prisoners' Chamber

Torture Chamber

Kitchens

Sleeping Quarters

Gunroom

Pages 30-31

Carilla knows that she must find five hidden number sequences to identify the stalls where Blondel will appear during the fair. First, she fills in the blanks on stalls where only one number is missing. Then, piecing this information together, she identifies two or three possible number sequnces for each of the four positions on the shields. Fitting these together, she arrives at the correct sequences. These are:

Left-hand shield, top: 1 4 7 10 13
Left-hand shield, bottom: 3 5 7 9 11
Right-hand shield, top: 10 12 14 16 18
Right-hand shield, bottom: 4 6 8 10 12
Flags: 17 38 71 116 173 (the difference between these numbers increases by 12 each time)

Blondel will therefore appear disguised as the following stallholders:
Day 1: Juggler
Day 2: The owner of the Dragon of Drumm
Day 3: The magician Mistoso
Day 4: The owner of Frommerty's Hearty Victuals
Day 5: Doctor Quack

Pages 32-33

From the information provided by the informer, Percival is able to deduce exactly what the villains are planning to do. They will board the steamer in the order CBDA. At the first meeting (8:05), C will hand the empty crate to B at place ✳. At the second meeting (8:15) D will hand the crate with the treasure to C at place Δ. At the third meeting (also 8:15), B will hand the empty crate to A at place □. At the fourth meeting (8:30) A will hand the empty crate to D at place M. Percival should therefore intercept the meeting at place Δ at 8:15.

Pages 34-35

From the secret notebook, Peg and Obadiah know that each of the nine hiding places on Cinnabar Island has been given a secret symbol and that the statue is hidden at place ⊕. Piecing together the information in the notebook, they match each hiding place to its symbol:

Palm Point is ⚒   The Great Falls are ⌐
The Wreck of the Buzzard is ♡   The Volcano is ⋀
The Jaggid Rocks are ◠   The Devil's Cave is ⟡
The Dolmen Stone is ⚲   The Blue Mountain is ⊕
The Watchtower is ⊖

The Calypso Figure is therefore hidden on the Blue Mountain.

Pages 36-37

First of all Skarpa names all the rooms in the fort:

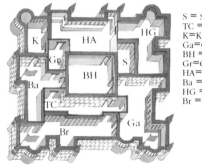

S = Sleeping Quarters
TC = Treasure Chamber
K = Kitchens
Ga = Guardsroom
BH = Banqueting Hall
Gr = Granary
HA = Hall of Axensord
Ba = Bakery
HG = Hall of Grendal
Br = Brewery

This is his route:
Br-Ba-K (during patrol 1); K-Gr (during patrol 2); Gr-BH (during patrol 3); BH-TC-Ba-K (during patrol 4); K-Gr (during patrol 5); Gr-Ba-Br (during patrol 6)

Pages 38-39

Freya knows that the casket is hidden in the Chamber of Gold and Rubies. To locate this room, she pieces together all the information on the right-hand side of the painting. This is what she discovers:

Kappa and the Chief of Ceremonies are playing chess in the Zebek Room
Gamma and the Poet are bathing in the Dragon Room
Tau and the Acrobat are dancing in the Djinni Room
Lambda and the Conjurer are reading in the Chamber of the Five Hundred Candles
Iota and the Grand Vizier are feasting in the Peacock Room
Bala and the Snake Charmer are playing music in the Chamber of Gold and Rubies

The Chamber of Gold and Rubies is therefore the room marked "Music" in the painting.

Pages 40-41

To find the statues, you must discover the moves that each of the seven pieces makes in the Games of Alfresco. To do this you need the following information: the statue of the god of poetry (also known as the Weather Charm of Wailen Valla) was stolen from Maelstrom, then later recovered by Skarpa the Bold; the statue of the god of dance (also known as the Calypso Figure) was stolen by pirates and recovered by Peg Traherne; the statue of the god of food (also known as the Epicurean Idol) fell into the hands of Horatio Faymus, then was stolen from Faymus Towers, later to be recovered by Percival Sharpe. From page 40, you also know that the statue of the god of music was hidden in the Amethyst Cave, then retrieved by Carilla di Galliard.
Remembering that only one piece may land on each square in the course of the game, and that all seven pieces finish on the same square, you can now deduce the moves for each piece:
Dance (made in Aluna Village): 4 24 27 30 33 35 43 47 58
Jests (made in Octana Village): 7 19 22 26 36 38 55 58
Poetry (made in Manzana Village): 5 8 11 18 20 53 58
Food (made in Samura Village): 2 28 31 34 37 39 45 50 58
Acrobatics (made in Agonda Village): 3 29 32 40 52 58
Drink (made in Azura Village): 10 14 15 48 51 54 58
Music (made in Nebula Village): 6 9 13 17 21 23 46 49 58
The statues are therefore hidden on Saskatoon Isle, which is shown on the map of Nathaniel Nanfresco on page 28.

First published in 1994 by Usborne Publishing Ltd, Usborne House, 83-85 Saffron Hill, London EC1N 8RT, England.
Copyright © 1994 Usborne Publishing Ltd.

The name Usborne and the device 🎈 are Trade Marks of Usborne Publishing Ltd.

Printed in Spain   U.E.
First published in America August 1994